# Henry Helps

## with

## Laundry

written by Beth Bracken     illustrated by Ailie Busby

PICTURE WINDOW BOOKS
a capstone imprint

Henry Helps books are published by Picture Window Books
A Capstone Imprint
1710 Roe Crest Drive
North Mankato, Minnesota 56003
www.capstonepub.com

Library of Congress Cataloging-in-Publication Data
Bracken, Beth.
Henry helps with laundry / by Beth Bracken ; illustrated by Ailie Busby.
p. cm. --  (Henry helps)
ISBN 978-1-4048-6772-7 (library binding)
ISBN 978-1-4048-7674-3 (paperback)
[1. Helpfulness--Fiction.] I. Busby, Ailie, ill. II. Title. III. Series.

PZ7.B6989Her 2011
[E]--dc22
2010050102


Graphic Designer: Russell Griesmer
Creative Director: Heather Kindseth
Production Specialist: Michelle Biedscheid


Printed in the United States of America in North Mankato, Minnesota.
012015
008704R

For Sam, the best helper I know. — BB

Everybody
in Henry's family
wears clothes.

Mom likes to wear boots and a skirt.

Dad likes to wear pants and a sweater.

Penny likes to wear pajamas.

And Henry likes to wear green shorts
and his octopus T-shirt.

Sometimes, clothes get dirty!

Henry is a good helper!

While Mom turns on the washing machine,
Henry sorts the clothes.

He puts the white clothes in one pile.
He puts the dark clothes in another pile.

Mom pours the soap in.

Henry puts the clothes in.

After Mom closes the lid,

Henry sees Penny's pajamas on the floor.

"Wait, Mom!" he yells.

"Don't forget to wash this!"

When the clothes are clean,

Henry and Mom put them in the dryer.

Finally, the clothes are dry.

Mom folds the clothes.

Henry carefully
puts them into piles.

Dad's clothes go in
Dad's dresser.

Mom's clothes go on
Mom's shelves.

Penny's clothes go in
Penny's room.

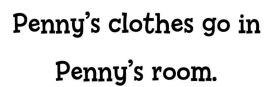

 Henry puts his clothes in his room.

What a good helper!